10th ANNIVERSARY EDITION

LIBRARY OF DOOM

ATTACK OF THE
PAPER BATS

by Michael Dahl
Illustrated by Martín Blanco

STONE ARCH BOOKS
a capstone imprint

Library of Doom is published by Stone Arch Books,
A Capstone imprint
1710 Roe Crest Drive
North Mankato, Minnesota 56003
www.mycapstone.com

Library of Congress Cataloging-in-Publication
Data is available on the Library of Congress
website.

ISBN: 978-1-4965-5531-1 (library binding)
ISBN: 978-1-4965-5537-3 (paperback)
ISBN: 978-1-4965-5543-4 (eBook PDF)

Summary: Will the Librarian be able to save the
day when a book transforms into a swarm of bats?

Designer: Brent Slingsby

Photo credits:
Design Element: Shutterstock: Shebeko.

Printed and bound in the USA.
010369F17

Table of Contents

The boy opens his window.

A small, dark shape falls out of the sky.

"Ow!" yells the boy. A sharp piece of paper slashes his hand.

THE LIBRARIAN

Real name: unknown
Parents: unknown
Birthplace/birthdate: unknown
Weaknesses: water, crumbs, dirty fingers
Strengths: speed reading, ability to fly,
martial arts

The Library

The Library of Doom is the world's largest collection of strange and dangerous books. Each generation, a new Librarian is chosen to serve as guardian. The Librarian's duty is to keep the books from falling into the hands of those who would use them for evil.

The location of the Library of Doom is unknown. Its shelves sit partially hidden underground. Some sections form a maze. It is full of black holes. This means someone might walk down a hallway in the Library and not realize they are traveling thousands of miles. One hallway could start somewhere under the Atlantic Ocean and end inside the caves of the Himalayas.

There are entries to the Library scattered all over the earth. But there are few exits. Sometimes villains find their way into the vast collection, but the Librarian always finds them out!

— From *The Atlas Cryptical*, compiled by Orson Drood, 5th official Librarian

CHAPTER ONE

THE BOOK LEFT OPEN

A book lies open on the street.

The book belongs to the Library of Doom. It was stolen from the Library many years ago.

It traveled through many lands, passing from person to person.

The breath of a thousand readers mixed with the ink and sighed through the paper.

———◆◆◆———

After many years, a young boy saw the book in the window of a small store.

"That's the book I want," said the boy.

As the boy hurried home with his new purchase, the book fell out of his bag.

Now, the book lies in the street.
Its pages grow **warm** in the pale
moonlight.

CHAPTER TWO

A STRANGE WIND

From out of nowhere, a cold wind blows down the street.

The wind shuffles the pages of the book. Several pages rip off.

The wind's invisible fingers fold and refold the pages into strange and deadly shapes.

The pages are sharp. The pages fly by themselves.

The pages are **hungry**.

On the **dark** street, the wind rips off more pages.

CHAPTER THREE

DARK WINDOWS

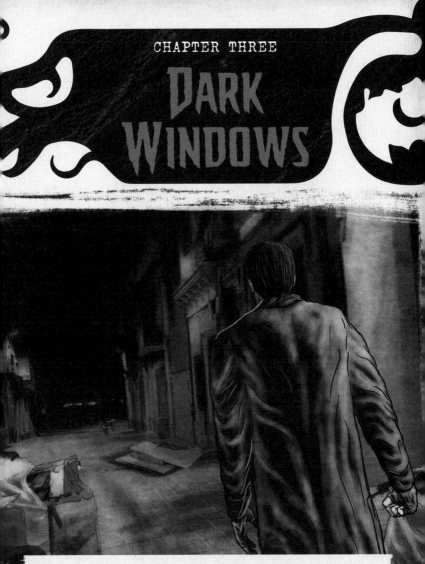

In another part of the dark city,
the Librarian walks alone.

The wind **whistles** down the street.

The Librarian pulls up his collar. He lowers his head as he walks into the wind.

As the Librarian stops in front of bookstores, he peers into the dark windows.

"None of these have the books I want," he whispers to himself.

The Librarian is searching
for books that were lost or stolen
from the Library of Doom.

A piece of paper flies overhead in
the wind.

A  **scream** rips through
the dark.

CHAPTER FOUR

THE SCREAM

In another street, a young boy
is reading a book.

He hears something scratch
softly against his window.

The boy opens his window.

A small, dark shape falls out of the sky.

"Ow!" yells the boy. A sharp piece of paper slashes his hand.

The boy tries to close the window,
but the wind is too strong. More
and more pieces of paper rush into
his room.

They move as if they were not
pieces of paper, but bats.

The boy **screams**.

CHAPTER FIVE

ATTACK!

The Librarian runs down a lonely alley.

He runs toward the sound of the scream.

Looking up, the Librarian sees
a cloud of pages.

Some of them are **flying** into
a small window high above him.

Somehow he must help the boy.

The Librarian leaps and grabs
the bottom of a fire escape. Quickly,
he darts up the metal stairway.

The Librarian crouches and then leaps. He flies across the alley.

As he leaps into the swarming ball of paper, the creatures attack.

He is surrounded.

The Librarian leans backward.
He loses his balance and **falls**
into the alley.

CHAPTER SIX

THE RIVER

The boy leans out his window.

He watches the paper bats leave his room and attack the man who tried to help him.

On the floor of the alley, the Librarian covers his head and face with his long, dark coat. Then he runs.

He cannot see where he is going, but he knows he cannot fight the swarm of pages.

The Librarian rushes down the alley. The alley drops off into a **dark river**.

The Librarian stops at the end
of the alley and then **dives**.

The pages dive after him.

In the water, the pages lose their sharp edges. The paper **falls apart.**

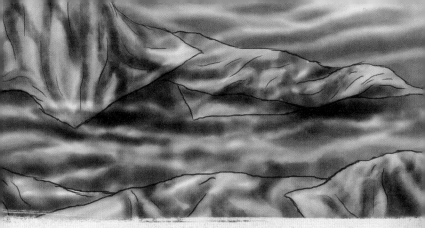

Everything sinks to the bottom of the river.

———◆◆———

In his room, the young boy looks through the closed window.

Where is the **strange** man who tried to rescue him?

THE END

NOTES FROM THE LIBRARIAN

The books stolen from the Library of Doom are dangerous and evil. Like other evil things, these books prefer the darkness. The darkness hides them, protects them, and often gives them power.

My hunt for these books takes me to many dark and forgotten corners of the world: dying cities, secluded small towns, graveyards, and empty deserts.

The book I hunted this time —
titled *Proteus* — was clever as well
as hungry. Each time the book attacked,
its pages turned into another shape.
Sometimes the pages became serpents
or cockroaches — or grinning masks
with teeth.

During the events in this
adventure, it was bats. Now the book's
pages are dissolved, and its cover lies
buried beneath a river. I won't reveal
the name of the river, but strangely
enough it rhymes with . . . "beast."

Paper

The word "paper" comes from "papyrus," a plant that grew along the Nile River in Egypt. Ancient Egyptians peeled strips from the tall plants and pounded them flat to write on.

Ts'ai Lun, a member of the Chinese emperor's court in 105 AD, is honored as the inventor of paper. He chopped up bamboo, bark from mulberry trees, and even fishing nets, to make a pulpy substance. When the pulp dried, it looked like our modern paper.

Today, paper is made from fibers that come mostly from trees, but can also come from straw or cotton.

Every year, the average student in the United States uses seven hundred pounds of paper!

Paper is dangerous! Brothers Homer and Langley Collyer never threw anything away. One day in 1947, they were found dead in their New York apartment buried under fallen stacks of old newspapers. It took rescuers eighteen days to recover the bodies from beneath all the paper.

ABOUT THE AUTHOR

Michael Dahl is the prolific author of the bestselling *Goodnight Baseball* picture book and more than two hundred other books for children and young adults. He has won the AEP Distinguished Achievement Award three times for his nonfiction, a Teachers' Choice Award from *Learning* magazine, and a Seal of Excellence from the Creative Child Awards. Dahl currently lives in Minneapolis, Minnesota.

ABOUT THE ILLUSTRATOR

Martín Blanco was born in Argentina and studied drawing and painting at the Fine Arts University of Buenos Aires. He is currently a freelance illustrator and lives in Barcelona, Spain, where he is working on films and comic books. Blanco loves to read, especially thrillers and horror. He also enjoys soccer, the Barcelona football team, and playing the drums with his friends.

GLOSSARY

dart (DART)—to move quickly

peer (PEER)—to stare or look carefully

shuffle (SHUF-uhl)—to move something quickly from one place to another; a person might shuffle through the pages of a phone book, searching for a certain telephone number

swarm (SWORM)—to move together in a big group; sharks swarm and so do bees

Discussion Questions

1. The boy who bought the book at the shop dropped it on his way home. Do you think that was an accident, or did something make the book fall out of his bag on purpose?

2. The Librarian used water to defeat the paper bats. How else do you think he could have defeated them?

3. Why do you think the Librarian was in the boy's city? What was he looking for? Use the text to support your answer.

WRITING PROMPTS

1. Write a paragraph about what happened to the boy after the paper bats left his room.

2. If you saw a cloud of paper bats flying toward you, what would you do? How would you escape them? Or would you stay and fight? Write down your adventure!

3. The boy was rescued by the Librarian. Write about a time when someone rescued you — or when you rescued someone else.

Building the Library

Some words from author Michael Dahl

One of my favorite writers is John Bellairs. In his spooky thriller, *The Dark Secret of Weatherend*, the heroes are attacked — by a swarm of dead leaves. The sharp dry leaves whirl around them, cutting their skin. What a scary scene! Those images were in my brain when I came up with the idea of paper turning into flying bats.

I knew the Librarian would be able to use water to defeat those bats. Because I once had my own terrifying experience with water and things flying through the air! I lived in South Carolina when it was hit by Hurricane Hugo. The powerful winds broke windows in my house. Rain poured in. Dozens and dozens of my books were completely soaked. I had to throw them all out. Water, I learned first-hand, was an enemy of the printed page. (It still bothers me that I had to throw away all those wonderful books.)